Sigmund

Watch Out for Joel!

Fly Trap

Cover illustration by Tammie Lyon
Cover design by Jennifer Parker

Published by Bethany House Publishers
A Ministry of Bethany Fellowship International
11400 Hampshire Avenue South
Bloomington, Minnesota 55438
www.bethanyhouse.com

Printed in China

Library of Congress Cataloging-in-Publication Data

Brouwer, Sigmund, 1959-
Fly trap / by Sigmund Brouwer.
p. cm. – (Watch out for Joel!)
Summary: While his older brother, Ricky, mixes cake for their mother's birthday, seven-year-old Joel plans to make an unusual present that involves flies, Popsicle sticks, and a camcorder.
ISBN 0-7642-2583-9
[1. Gifts—Fiction. 2. Birthdays—Fiction. 3. Christian life—Fiction.] I. Title.
II. Series: Brouwer, Sigmund, 1959- . Watch out for Joel!
PZ7.B79984Fl 2003
[E]—dc21 2002010734

Love One Another

Joel wants to make a birthday present for his mom. Will she be happy with what he makes?

John 13:34 says, "I give you a new command: Love each other. You must love each other as I have loved you." Ricky and Joel want to do something special for their mom. As you read the story, can you think of a time when you did something special for someone else?

1

Joel walked into the kitchen with a large jar that was filled with flies.

Joel's older brother, Ricky, stood at the kitchen table. He was mixing a big bowl of cake batter.

Their big dog stood there in the kitchen, too, waiting to lick some cake batter. Their dog's name was Boo-Boo.

"I am making a cake for Mom's birthday tomorrow," Ricky said to Joel. "And I already bought her a present. What are you going to do for her birthday?"

"Yes, tomorrow is Mom's birthday," Joel said. "I will give her a present, too."

Joel showed Ricky the glass jar filled with flies. Joel had caught twenty flies and put them in the jar. There was a lid on the jar. The flies inside were big. They buzzed loudly.

Ricky looked at the glass jar with flies.

"You are going to give her a jar of flies for her present?" Ricky asked.

"No," Joel said. "Just wait and see."

Joel walked to the fridge. He put the flies in the freezer.

"You are going to give her a jar of frozen flies?" Ricky laughed at his younger brother. "Is that what you give for presents when you are only seven years old?"

Joel smiled.

"Just wait and see," Joel said.

2

Joel had two Popsicle sticks in his back pocket. He took the Popsicle sticks out of his pocket. He put the Popsicle sticks on the kitchen table near where Ricky was mixing the cake.

Boo-Boo, their big dog, stood there by the table, too, waiting to lick some cake batter.

"What are those?" Ricky asked Joel when he saw the Popsicle sticks.

"Popsicle sticks," Joel said. "Don't you

know? You are thirteen. You said you know everything."

"I *know* those are Popsicle sticks," Ricky said. "What I want to know is why you have them."

"Tomorrow is Mom's birthday," Joel said. "I want to give her a present."

"You are going to give her Popsicle sticks?" Ricky laughed at his younger brother. "Is that what you give for presents when you are only seven years old?"

Joel smiled.

"Just wait and see," Joel said.

3

Joel had a bottle of glue in his other back pocket. He put that on the kitchen table near where Ricky was mixing the cake.

Boo-Boo, their big dog, stood there by the table, too, waiting to lick some cake batter.

"What is that?" Ricky asked Joel when he saw the bottle of glue on the table beside the Popsicle sticks.

"A bottle of glue," Joel said. "Don't you know? You are thirteen. You said you know everything."

"I *know* it is a bottle of glue," Ricky said.

"What I want to know is why you have it."

Joel had a pair of tweezers in his front pocket. He put the tweezers on the kitchen table near where Ricky was mixing the cake.

"What is that?" Ricky asked Joel when he saw the tweezers beside the bottle of glue and the Popsicle sticks.

"A pair of tweezers," Joel said. "Don't you know? You are thirteen. You said you know everything."

"I *know* those are tweezers," Ricky said. "What I want to know is why you have them."

"Tomorrow is Mom's birthday," Joel said. "I want to give her a present."

"You are going to give her a bottle of glue and some tweezers?" Ricky asked. Ricky laughed at his younger brother. "Is that what you give for presents when you are only seven years old?"

Joel smiled.

"Just wait and see," Joel said.

4

Joel left the kitchen for a few minutes. Ricky kept stirring the bowl of cake batter. It was a big bowl and needed a lot of stirring.

Boo-Boo, their big dog, stood there by the table, too, waiting to lick some cake batter.

Finally, Joel came back.

Joel had the family camcorder. Joel put that on the kitchen table beside the Popsicle sticks and the bottle of glue and the tweezers.

"What is that?" Ricky asked Joel when he saw the camcorder beside the tweezers and

the bottle of glue and the Popsicle sticks.

"A camcorder," Joel said. "Don't you know? You are thirteen. You said you know everything."

"I *know* it is a camcorder," Ricky said. "What I want to know is why you have it."

"Tomorrow is Mom's birthday," Joel said. "I want to give her a present."

"You are going to give her a camcorder?" Ricky asked.

"No," Joel said. "I am going to give her a video."

"A video?" Ricky asked. Ricky laughed at his younger brother. "Is that what you give for presents when you are only seven years old?"

Joel smiled.

"Just wait and see," Joel said.

5

Joel stood at the kitchen table. Joel took the bottle of glue. Joel took the Popsicle sticks. Joel glued one Popsicle stick on top of the other in the shape of a T.

Joel put twenty little dabs of glue across the top of one of the Popsicle sticks.

"What are you doing?" Ricky asked Joel.

Boo-Boo, their big dog, stood there by the table, too, waiting to lick some cake batter.

"Don't you know?" Joel said. "You are thirteen. You said you know everything. I am putting little dabs of glue on the Popsicle stick."

"I know you are putting little dabs of glue on the Popsicle stick," Ricky said. "I want to know why you are doing that."

"Tomorrow is Mom's birthday," Joel said. "I want to give her a present."

"You are going to give her Popsicle sticks with glue?" Ricky asked. Ricky laughed at his younger brother. "Is that what you give for presents when you are only seven years old?"

Joel smiled.

"Just wait and see," Joel said.

6

Joel went to the freezer and pulled out his jar of flies. The flies were so cold they could barely move.

Joel brought the jar of flies to the kitchen table.

Boo-Boo, their big dog, stood there by the table, too, waiting to lick some cake batter.

Joel took the lid off the jar. The flies did not fly out. They were so cold they could barely move.

Joel took the tweezers. Joel reached into the jar with the tweezers. Joel grabbed a fly

with the tweezers. Joel held the fly by its wing. Joel was careful not to hurt the fly. Joel lifted the fly out of the jar. Joel stuck the fly's legs to one of the dabs of glue.

"What are you doing?" Ricky asked Joel.

"Don't you know?" Joel said. "You are thirteen. You said you know everything. I am gluing the fly by its legs to the Popsicle stick."

"I *know* you are gluing the fly by its legs to the Popsicle stick," Ricky said. "I want to know why you are doing that."

"Tomorrow is Mom's birthday," Joel said. "I want to give her a present."

"You are going to give her a Popsicle stick with a fly glued to it?" Ricky laughed at his younger brother. "Is that what you give for presents when you are only seven years old?"

Joel smiled.

"Just wait and see," Joel said.

7

Joel glued all twenty of the flies across the top of the Popsicle stick. The flies were so cold they could barely move.

Joel lifted the camcorder from the table. He pointed the camcorder at the Popsicle stick with the twenty flies glued to it.

Boo-Boo, their big dog, stood there by the table, too, waiting to lick some cake batter.

"What are you doing?" Ricky asked.

"Don't you know?" Joel said. "You are thirteen. You said you know everything. I am using this camcorder to make a video of the

flies on the Popsicle sticks."

"I know you are using that camcorder to make a video of the flies on the Popsicle sticks," Ricky said. "I want to know why you are doing that."

"Tomorrow is Mom's birthday," Joel said. "I want to give her a present."

"You are going to give Mom a video of flies glued to two Popsicle sticks?" Ricky laughed at his younger brother. "Is that what you give for presents when you are only seven years old?"

Joel smiled.

"Just wait and see," Joel said.

8

Joel kept pointing the camcorder at the twenty flies that were glued to the two Popsicle sticks.

Boo-Boo, their big dog, stood there by the table, too, waiting to lick some cake batter.

Soon, the flies began to get warm. Soon, the flies began to buzz. Soon, the flies began to flap their wings. Soon, the flies began to try to fly.

But the legs of all the flies were stuck to the Popsicle sticks by glue.

So the flies were stuck.

They flapped their wings *really* hard.

They buzzed *really* hard.

Joel kept pointing his camcorder at the flies that were stuck to the Popsicle sticks.

When all of the flies were warm again and when all of the flies were buzzing loudly, something strange happened.

Because all of their legs were stuck to the Popsicle sticks, all of the flies together began to lift the sticks into the air.

"See!" Joel said to Ricky. "It is a fly-powered Popsicle-stick airplane!"

The fly-powered Popsicle-stick airplane flew through the air.

Joel kept pointing the camcorder at the fly-powered airplane.

"See!" Joel said to Ricky. "I want to give Mom a video that will make her laugh. That will be a nice present."

9

Boo-Boo, their big dog, saw the fly-powered Popsicle-stick airplane.

Boo-Boo began to bark at the fly-powered Popsicle-stick airplane.

Boo-Boo began to chase the fly-powered Popsicle-stick airplane.

Joel kept pointing the camcorder. Joel kept taking a video. He thought it would be a funny video to give his mom as a present.

Ricky chased Boo-Boo to make Boo-Boo quiet.

It didn't work.

Ricky tripped over Boo-Boo.

Ricky fell into the kitchen table.

The kitchen table fell.

It fell on Ricky.

So did the cake bowl with all the cake batter.

It fell on Ricky's head.

Finally, Boo-Boo got to lick some of the cake batter.

Joel kept pointing the camcorder. Joel put all of this on video.

And the next day, he gave the video to his mom as a birthday present.

When she saw it, she laughed very hard.

When she saw it, she laughed very long.

"Thank you, Joel," she said. "That was a nice present."

Joel thought it was, too.

Joel really liked the part where Boo-Boo licked cake batter from Ricky's head.

A Lesson About Love

In *Fly Trap*, Ricky and Joel make presents for their mom's birthday because they love her.

Love is important. God says that we need to love each other the same way that He has loved us. There are many simple ways to show love to others, like Joel and Ricky showed love to their mom.

To Talk About

1. How does God show His love to us?
2. Who do you know who is in special need of love today?
3. What can you do to show God's love to others?

"I tell you, we should all love each other. This is not a new command. It is the same command we have had from the beginning."
2 John 1:5b

Award-winning author Sigmund Brouwer inspires kids to love reading. From WATCH OUT FOR JOEL! to the ACCIDENTAL DETECTIVES series (full of stories about Joel's older brother, Ricky), Sigmund writes books that kids want to read again and again. Not only does he write cool books, Sigmund also holds writing camps and classes for more than ten thousand children each year!

You can read more about Sigmund, his books, and the Young Writer's Institute on his Web site, *www.coolreading.com*.